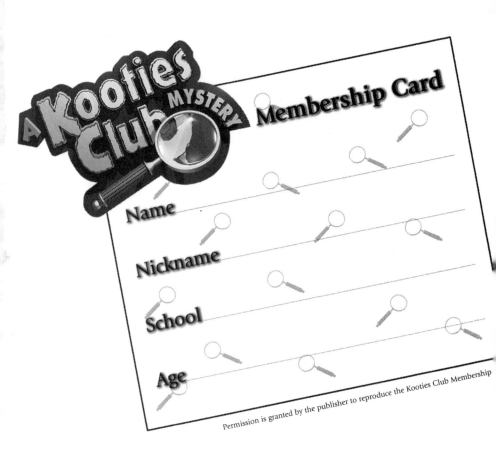

A Kooties Club MYSTERY

Membership Card

Name

Nickname

School

Age

Table of Contents

Introduction

Abe, Ben, Gabe, Toby, and Ty live in a large city. There isn't much for kids to do. There isn't even a park close by.

Their neighborhood is made up of
apartment houses and trailer parks.
Gas stations and small shops stand
where the parks and grass used to be.
And there aren't many houses with
big yards.

Ty and Abe live in an apartment complex. Next door is a large vacant lot. It is full of brush, weeds, and trash. A path runs across the lot. On the other side is a trailer park. Ben and Toby live there.

Across the street from the trailer park is a big gray house. Gabe lives in the top apartment of the house.

The five boys have known each other since they started school. But they haven't always been friends.

The other kids say the boys have cooties. And the other kids won't touch them with a ten-foot pole. So Abe, Ben, Gabe, Toby, and Ty have formed their own club. They call it the Kooties Club.

Here's how to join. If no one else will have anything to do with you, you're in.

The boys call themselves the Koots for short. Ben's grandma calls his grandpa an *old coot*. And Ben thinks his grandpa is pretty cool. So if he's an old coot, Ben and his friends must be young koots.

The Koots play ball and hang out with each other. But most of all, they look for mysteries to solve.

Chapter 1

Nothing to Do

The Koots kicked the ball around the parking lot. Gabe kicked the ball to Ben. Thud! Ben hit the ball with his head. It went to Abe. Wham! Abe kicked the ball to Ty. Thud! Ty hit the ball with the side of his leg. It went to Toby. Whoosh! Toby missed. The ball rolled past him.

"Rats!" said Toby. "It went under a car again." He ran to get the ball.

10

"I wish we had a better place to play," Ben said. "This parking lot is bad. Too many cars and no grass."

Just then a car backed out of a parking place. The Koots ran for the curb.

"I know," said Ty, "but it's the biggest place we have."

"I wish I had a big yard," said Abe.

"Then you'd be rich," Ben replied. "And you'd find new friends."

"No way!" said Abe. "When I'm rich, you'll still be my friends."

"When you're rich, Abe, get a pool," said Ty. "Then I'll still be your friend!"

"I got the ball," said Toby, coming from under the car.

11

"Let's do something else," Ben said. "I'm not good at this." He sat down on the grass between the parking lot and the sidewalk.

"If we don't play ball, what can we do?" asked Gabe as he sat down next to Ben. He lay back on the grass and looked up at the sky.

The other Koots joined Gabe and Ben. They all lay back and looked up at the sky.

They saw gray clouds. Rain was coming. The Koots tried to think of something to do.

Ty looked up at building A across the parking lot. He lived in building B. He lived in apartment B-8 on the second floor.

12

Abe lived in building B too. He lived in apartment B-3 on the first floor. Building B faced building A. The parking lot was between them.

Abe's apartment was bigger than Ty's. His family had to fit both parents, both grandparents, Abe, and his little sister in the apartment.

Ty only had his mom and older brother. Ty shared his bedroom with his brother. But his brother only came home to sleep and eat.

Ty knew all the people in the apartments. If he didn't know their names, he knew their faces. He also knew which cars they drove. And he knew who was in each family. He even knew which apartment each family lived in.

13

A funny look crossed Ty's face. He asked Abe, "Do you know who lives in apartment A-13? I've never seen anyone."

"No," said Abe. "It's always dark at night. Maybe it's empty."

"I don't think so," said Ty. "Every day some lady or man brings a sack. They don't stay long. And they have a sack when they leave. Someone has to be in there."

"I have a great idea!" said Gabe. He patted himself on the back. "Let's spy on apartment A-13!"

Chapter 2

The Spies

Ty pointed to apartment A-13. It was on the third floor. There was a small window, a big window, and a small porch with a door.

"That apartment is just like mine," said Ty. "I can tell by the windows."

"So what if we know about the rooms?" asked Toby. "What good will that do us? How can we spy on an apartment that's on the third floor?"

"If nothing ever happens, what can we spy on?" asked Ben.

"That's the fun!" said Gabe. He sat up. "It will be hard to spy on an apartment on the third floor. And it will be hard to spy on one where nothing ever happens. We'll have to use our heads."

"It'll be just like in the movies," said Ty. He was getting excited now. "We'll set up a base in my bedroom. We can see A-13 from my window."

The boys ran to Ty's apartment. They went into his bedroom. Then they looked out his window.

Ty's window faced building A. The boys had to look up and a little to the left to see A-13.

The Koots sat together by the window. They looked at apartment A-13. Nothing happened. They kept watching. Still nothing happened.

"This is boring," Ben said.

"We have to think of a better way to spy," said Toby.

"OK, here's what we'll do," answered Gabe.

Chapter 3

Gabe's Plan

The Koots gathered around Gabe and listened to his plan.

"Ty, you keep watching. Even at night when you're in bed. Abe, you do the same. But we need to hear what's going on in the apartment too. We need to listen at the door."

"I don't want to do that," said Abe. He took a couple of steps back from the group.

"Me neither," said Toby.

"Count me out!" said Ben.

"OK, then. Ty and I will listen. You guys stay here and watch. Come on, Ty," said Gabe.

Ty and Gabe stopped in the kitchen and got two glasses.

"We can hold these up to the door. They'll help us hear what's happening on the other side of the door," said Ty. "I saw this on TV."

Ty and Gabe walked across the parking lot. Ben, Abe, and Toby watched from Ty's window. Ty and Gabe went into building A. The three boys in the window couldn't see them anymore.

Ty and Gabe didn't want to be noticed. So they used the stairs instead of the elevator.

The boys climbed to the third floor. They walked very slowly. They tiptoed down the hall. Ty and Gabe stopped in front of apartment A-13. They looked around. Nobody was coming.

The boys pulled the glasses from under their jackets. They put the glasses up to the door. Each boy put an ear against the bottom of his glass.

Then they heard it!

Ty and Gabe looked at each other. Their mouths dropped open. And their eyes got bigger.

The boys took off. They ran all the way down the stairs and out the door. They flew across the parking lot. They rushed into Ty's apartment and locked the door. Then they ran into the bedroom.

Ty and Gabe slammed the bedroom door shut. They leaned against the door. Both boys were panting.

Ben, Abe, and Toby had watched their two friends running across the lot. Now they just stared at them.

"You both look like you've seen a ghost," said Ben.

Chapter 4

Strange Noises

"Did you hear what I heard?" whispered Ty. He stared at Gabe. His eyes were still big. And he was breathing fast.

"I think so," answered Gabe. His eyes were big too. And he was breathing fast. "I heard yelling and screaming. And someone was laughing. Someone very bad."

"Yes," said Ty. "Someone evil was laughing. And someone was screaming. Something terrible is happening in that apartment!"

"Oh, it's just something on TV," laughed Toby. "Let's go turn on the TV. You'll see."

The boys went into the living room. Ty turned on the TV. He flipped through the channels. There was nothing. Nothing was on TV that was like what Ty and Gabe had heard.

"I don't want to go back," said Ty.

"Me neither," said Gabe, shaking his head. He looked at Ben, Toby, and Abe. "Why don't you guys go listen?"

"Do you want to?" asked Ben, looking at the others.

25

"No way!" answered Toby and Abe at the same time.

"Me neither," said Ben. He looked at Gabe and Ty. "We believe you. You guys really looked scared!"

"What should we do now?" asked Ty. "Something is wrong. Very wrong."

"Let's keep watching for now," Toby suggested.

So the boys sat and watched. Other people came and went. But no one came out of or went into apartment A-13.

It was getting late. Almost time for supper. People began turning on their lights.

Suddenly a strange car parked below Ty's window. A man got out.

26

He was carrying a sack. He went into building A.

A short time later, the man returned to his car. But now he was carrying a different sack. He got into his car and drove off.

"There!" shouted Abe. "I know I've seen that man before. He doesn't live here, does he, Ty?"

"No," said Ty. "He dropped off something at A-13. Then he took something away."

"That sack was too small to hold a body," said Ben.

"Maybe it's just the head and the fingertips," said Gabe. "Without those, the cops can't make an I.D. The rest of the body could be in the trash. Tomorrow, we'll check the dumpster."

"It's time for dinner. I need to go home," Gabe added. "Want to walk with me, Ben? Toby?"

"Sure," said Ben. "It's getting dark out."

"You guys keep watching apartment A-13," Toby said as the three boys left for home.

Chapter 5

The Stranger

Ty lay on his bed. He looked out the window at apartment A-13.

Downstairs, Abe lay on his bed. He watched A-13 too.

Apartment A-13 was dark. Lights were on in other apartments. But not A-13.

What was going on in apartment A-13? At last, Ty fell asleep. But Abe didn't. Abe kept watching.

Rain had started. It was pouring. The parking lot had a spooky look to it. Everything seemed to move like ghosts.

Suddenly a man came out of building A. He didn't live in any of the apartments.

The man walked quickly through the rain. He had a basket of clothes.

"Could a body be in the clothes?" thought Abe.

The man crossed the parking lot. He walked close to Abe's window. He slowed down and turned his head. He looked right at Abe as he passed. He looked evil.

"Oh, no! He's seen me!" Abe said to himself. "I'm dead!" Abe shut the drapes. He didn't go to sleep for a long, long time.

Who was that man? What was really in the basket?

When he did fall asleep, Abe had bad dreams. He dreamed the man came into his room. He had a big knife. He tried to dice Abe into small pieces and stuff him into the basket.

"Abe, wake up! You're screaming!" said Abe's little sister Kim. Abe shared a room with her.

"Do you want me to get Mom?" asked Kim.

"No," Abe answered. "I know! Let's trade beds. You can have the window. I'll take the wall."

"Okay!" said Kim. She liked that idea.

Abe got into the other bed. But he didn't sleep well the rest of the night.

The next day in school, Abe could hardly keep his eyes open. At lunch, he told the Koots what had happened.

"He could have been anybody," Gabe said.

"Yes. But he came from building A. And I didn't know him. He looked so evil," said Abe. He looked around the room at the other kids.

Abe lowered his voice and leaned closer to the Koots. "I have to tell you, I'm really scared."

"Stick with me when we go home," said Ty. "Tell me if you see him again. We'll follow him."

"No way!" said Abe. "You can follow him yourself!"

Ignoring Abe, Ty said, "OK, guys. Meet at my house after school. And we'll check the dumpster."

Everybody nodded.

Chapter 6

The Stranger Returns

The dumpster was full of sacks. And they all looked alike. Gabe pulled one out and opened it. It had food scraps and junk in it. He pulled out another. Garbage. The other boys watched him.

Turning up his nose, Ty said, "I don't want to look through the trash."

Ben added, "I don't want to find body parts."

"There has to be a better way," Toby said. "Let's go back to Ty's and think about it."

Just then Gabe jumped up from the sacks of garbage, waving something in the air. "Here's a bone!" he said excitedly.

Toby looked at it. "That's from a steak, dummy. You can tell. It's been cut."

"So maybe that's what we heard," said Gabe. "Somebody was being cut up." He made sawing movements with his right hand across his left arm.

The other Koots shook their heads. They walked back to Ty's apartment. Gabe was still looking in the trash. Finally, he followed the others.

Back at Ty's window, the group waited and watched.

"I wish we could wire that apartment for sound," said Ben. "Then we could hear without being too close."

"Only the cops can do that," said Toby. "That's what I heard on TV."

"Maybe we should call the cops," offered Abe.

"What would we say?" asked Gabe. "We don't have any proof. They won't do anything if we can't find a body."

Just then a car parked outside. It was the same man Abe had seen the night before.

The man carried another sack. He entered building A.

"Let's follow him!" said Gabe.

All the boys ran outside. Gabe and Ty led the others. Abe, Toby, and Ben hung back a little. By the time they reached the elevator, the man was already on his way up. "You guys wait here!" shouted Gabe. "Watch him when he comes down. And call the cops if we don't come back!" Ty and Gabe took the stairs, two steps at a time.

Abe and Toby hid around the corner from the elevator. Ben stood outside. It seemed like they waited a long time. They were worried about Gabe and Ty.

At last the man came down. Abe and Toby watched him go out the front door. He had another sack in his hand.

38

Outside, Ben saw the man hurry to his car. He put the sack in the trunk. He closed the trunk quickly. But not before Ben saw other sacks in the trunk.

The man glanced around to see if anyone was watching. Ben ducked behind a bush. Quickly, the man jumped into his car and drove off.

Ben went back inside building A. The three boys met by the elevator.

"That man is up to something bad," Ben said. "He was trying to hide the sacks. But I saw lots of them in his trunk."

The three waited for Ty and Gabe. They waited and waited.

"We'd better call the cops," said Abe.

39

Just then, Ty and Gabe came down the stairs.

"Well," said Ty. "Something strange is going on. Something very strange. Let's go back to my room. Maybe we can figure it out."

Chapter 7

Mel Sonwell?

When they got back, Gabe told the others what had happened. "We waited down the hall. But there was no place to hide. So Ty and I acted like we had just knocked on A-10's door. And we were waiting for it to open."

Gabe continued, "The man got out of the elevator. He knocked on A-13's door. It seemed like he waited forever for someone to open the door."

"It was hard," added Ty. "We were waiting too. It seemed funny for all of us to be waiting."

"The man looked at us," said Gabe. "He looked really mean."

"Finally," said Ty, "someone opened the door to apartment A-13."

"Who was it? Did you see anyone?" asked Ben. He leaned closer to Gabe and Ty.

"We couldn't see," said Ty, shaking his head. "It was dark in the apartment. The man gave the sack to someone. And he got a sack back."

"Did he say anything?" asked Toby.

Gabe answered, "I think he said, 'Mel Sonwell. Betsy will be by tomorrow.' Then the door shut."

"He had to pass us to get to the elevator. He looked right at us," said Ty. "And he didn't smile."

"Mel Sonwell must be his name. I think it's the mob," said Toby.

"I think they're spies," said Ben. "He was using code."

"We should call the cops," said Abe nervously.

"I have an idea," Toby said. "Give me some time to work it out in my head. Then I'll tell you about it tomorrow."

Toby left to form his plan. The other guys sat watching apartment A-13 from Ty's window. Something bad was going on behind those walls. But what could it be?

Chapter 8

Toby's Plan

After school the next day, the Koots were in the parking lot. They kicked the ball to each other. Toby had shared his idea. And this was part of the plan.

Ty kicked the ball to Ben. Whap! Ben kicked the ball to Gabe. Thud! Gabe kicked the ball to Abe. Wham! Abe kicked the ball to Toby. Toby caught the ball with his hands. Then he tried for a three-story basket. He missed.

So they started over. Ty kicked the ball to Ben. Thud! Ben kicked the ball to Gabe. Wham! Gabe kicked the ball to Abe. Whap! Abe kicked the ball to Toby. Again Toby caught the ball with his hands. Again he tried for a three-story basket. This time he made it!

The boys stood in the parking lot. They stared up at the porch of apartment A-13. No one came out to throw their ball back. The boys stood and waited.

A car drove into the parking lot. A lady with a sack got out. That was Ty and Gabe's cue. Time for part two of Toby's plan.

The two boys ran for building A. They ran up the stairs to the third floor.

The lady took the elevator. When she reached apartment A-13, Ty and Gabe were waiting.

"We lost our ball on this person's porch," said Gabe. "We'd like to get it back."

"How did your ball get up to the third floor?" asked the lady. She stared at both boys.

"We were seeing how high we could kick it," said Ty. He was shaking. So was Gabe.

The lady turned back to the door. She knocked.

Ty, Gabe, and the lady waited. They waited for a long time. The lady knocked again.

At last, the door opened slowly. The room inside was dark. The boys

46

couldn't see anyone or anything.

"Hello, Mr. Dodge. You have some visitors tonight," said the lady cheerfully. She handed Mr. Dodge her sack. Mr. Dodge handed her another sack.

"Come right on in," said Mr. Dodge in a gruff voice. Ty and Gabe stepped into the darkness.

"See you tomorrow, Mr. Dodge," the lady said. She turned and headed for the elevator.

The door shut behind Ty and Gabe. They were left alone in the dark with Mr. Dodge. Whoever Mr. Dodge was!

Toby's plan had backfired. The lady had not saved them from the evil inside apartment A-13.

Chapter 9

Help Arrives

Ben, Toby, and Abe waited in the parking lot. They looked up at the porch of apartment A-13. They could see the ball. But that was all.

Nobody came out to get the ball. Nobody even looked out the window. Nothing changed.

The boys kept waiting.

After a while, the lady came downstairs. She was alone.

But the lady had another sack in her hands. She put the sack into her trunk and got into the car. She backed out and quickly drove away.

Toby read the license plate number. AGR 447.

"AGR 447," said Toby. "Let's go write it down."

"Yes," said Abe. "We can give it to the cops."

They ran to Abe's apartment. Abe wrote down the number. Then he dialed 911.

Abe told the man on the line what had happened. The man asked a lot of questions. Finally, he told Abe someone would be right over. The man said Abe should wait outside for the officer.

Abe, Ben, and Toby went outside to wait. They looked up at the porch of apartment A-13. A light was on in the apartment! They could see a shadow on the curtain! It was getting bigger. No, now it was getting smaller.

Someone was moving around inside. What was going on? What had happened to Ty and Gabe? Were they still alive? Would the boys ever see them again?

Just then a police car pulled up. The officer stepped out.

"Which one of you is Abe?" asked the officer.

"I am, ma'am," said Abe.

"I'm Officer Marks. Do you live around here?" she asked.

"Yes. Right there in apartment B-3," replied Abe.

"Well, what's going on, Abe?" asked Officer Marks.

Abe pointed to apartment A-13 and told the story.

"Let's go knock on the door and see what your friends are up to," the officer said.

She and the three boys walked into building A.

Chapter 10

Apartment A-13

Officer Marks knocked on the door of apartment A-13. The door opened slowly. Ty was standing there. He had a funny look on his face.

"What is going on here?" asked Officer Marks.

"Nothing, ma'am," said Ty. "Everything is fine."

A strange laugh and screams could be heard.

"See, we told you strange things were going on in there," the other boys said at once.

"What is that noise?" asked the officer.

"Oh, that's nothing," answered Ty. "Just Mr. Dodge's book on tape."

"May we come in?" Officer Marks asked.

"Mr. Dodge, you have more visitors," Ty said. "May they come in?"

"Yes," said the gruff voice.

The new visitors entered the apartment. Gabe was sitting in a chair. Next to him sat a man in a wheelchair. They were listening to a tape player.

"Are those the screams you boys heard?" asked Officer Marks.

54

"Sure are!" said Gabe.

"I like mysteries," said Mr. Dodge. "But I'm blind. So I can't read. Therefore, I get books on tape."

He went on. "Otherwise, my life is quiet and dark. I can't see. So I don't turn on a light. It does me no good."

"Then who is Mel Sonwell? What happened to him?" Toby asked.

"Mel Sonwell?" asked Mr. Dodge. A puzzled look crossed his face. Then his face cleared.

Mr. Dodge laughed. "You must mean Meals on Wheels! They bring my supper every night. Then they take my trash away for me.

"Sometimes they pick up my laundry. Later, they bring it back," he continued.

55

"Any other questions?" asked Mr. Dodge.

"Yes," said Ty. "Could we visit you sometime? We'd like to listen to a book on tape too."

"Sure," laughed Mr. Dodge. "We'll turn out the lights and have a good scare."